Whipping As A Fine Art

*being an Account of exquisite and refined
Chastisement inflicted
by Mr. Howard on grown-up
Schoolgirls.*

BY

CHARLES SACKVILLE

AUTHOR OF

"Maud Cameron and her Guardian,"
"Mr. Howard Goes Yachting," "Fantastic Chastisements,"
and "Two Lascivious Adventures."

———

PRICE £ 1.10.0

LONDON and PARIS
MCMIX

———

BIRCHGROVE PRESS
MMXII

Whipping as a Fine Art is one of a series of clandestine Edwardian novels attributed to Charles Sackville following the sexual adventures of Mr. Howard, a young but ferocious disciplinarian in the mould of despotic Victorian fictional flagellants such as Colonel Spanker (*Experimental Lecture by Colonel Spanker*) and Sir Charles Dacre (*The Pleasures of Cruelty*). Like most of the Sackville books, it was probably issued by Roberts and Dardaillon, Charles Carrington's agents in Paris during his period in Brussels (c. 1907-1912). *Whipping as a Fine Art* was first published c. 1909 in a limited edition of two hundred and fifty copies, *"issued to Subscribers Only."*

'Charles Sackville' is a pseudonym; it is not known who wrote the books attributed to him. Bibliographer Peter Mendes suggests (without supporting argumentation) that they 'were probably written by Carrington himself'. (*Clandestine Erotic Fiction in English 1800-1930 A bibliographical study.* Aldershot: Scolar Press, 1993, p. 36)

Other Charles Sackville titles include: *Maud Cameron and her Guardian* (1903), *Two Lascivious Adventures of Mr. Howard* (1907), *Mr. Howard Goes Yachting* (1907), *Three Chapters in the Life of Mr. Howard* (1908), *The Amazing Chastisements of Miss Bostock* (1908), *Fantastic Chastisements* (1908), and *Exquisite Castigation* (1909).

WHIPPING AS A FINE ART

PREFACE

PREFACE

This delightful volume describes the chastisement of a grown-up young lady in the school that Mr. Howard's nieces manage for his amusement. She is detected in having written a very indiscreet manuscript and Mr. Howard takes her punishment in hand himself. The girl, being very beautiful, Mr. Howard allows his imagination full play in inventing the most prolonged and excruciating punishments, stripping her naked and fastening her with straps in startling contortions in which to receive her chastisements.

The sensual excitement he derives from treating the lovely, modest young lady in the most outrageously indecent manner, impels him to inflict a fierce and prolonged flogging upon her helpless, struggling naked limbs and body.

This book is another masterpiece of scientific refined voluptuousness, proving once more that Mr. Charles Sackville has no equal or rival in this branch of literature.

He promises the publisher that this volume shall be followed with one more which will complete and exhaust the entire range of sensual possibilities arising from the art and practice of chastising young ladies.

———

CHAPTER I

Whipping
As A Fine Art

CHAPTER I

Maud brought to Mr. Howard a Ms.
which she found secreted in Mary Hullah's
drawer. It was in her own hand-writing, but
whether it was entirely a work of
imagination or was founded upon some
personal knowledge, she would not reveal.
However, it served Mr. Howard in two
ways, first as an amusing pastime to peruse,
and secondly, as a reason for inflicting a
very severe whipping upon Miss Hullah.
The Ms. began by describing how a curate

and his wife increased their slender income by taking in girls as boarders, from which innocent beginning they both soon developed a most reprehensible habit of chastising the lasses ostensibly for their good, but really because it gave the couple lascivious pleasure. At first the lady whipped the girls by herself, but by degrees the curate assisted; the girls being previously blindfolded.

One day in the summer, during his rounds, the curate sat under a hedge to rest and two lovers happened to come close to him on the other side of it, where, as lovers will, they got more and more loving and familiar. The curate, tempted beyond power of resistance, crept to a position where he could hear and see all that passed. He watched the man gradually uncovering the girl's breasts for his wanton feelings, and then the lifting of the frothy petticoats; the exposure of the dainty drawers and slim legs; the faint resistance of the panting girl; the firm insistence of the lusty swain and final abandoned ecstasy of the hot lovers; the last plunge of passion and the swoon of ultimate satisfaction. The Ms. then continued:

The curate, after seeing all this, hastened home intent upon enjoying himself with the punishment of one of his pupils, but as luck would have it, something even more delectable was awaiting him. His wife's niece was staying in the house and his better half would never allow him to chastise her or be present when she found it her duty to do so. This only made him more eager to compass it somehow.

For this purpose, he had placed the girl who was under sixteen, in a bedroom that had a balcony which he could easily reach from his study window. Often he would peep at night between the blind and the sash and enjoy watching her undress, but she always put on her nightdress over her chemise so that he saw only enough to make him long to see more. He felt that until he could strip her for a whipping he would never see her properly. On reaching home about ten o'clock, he saw a light from her window. Slipping quietly up, he peeped in and saw her reclining in the arm-chair before the fire in her chemise and drawers doing with one of her hands what she had no business to be doing.

At last, he thought he had his opportunity. He tried the window gently and found it unfastened. In a moment he had opened it and stepped in. It was a French window to the ground.

The girl hurriedly flung her dressing-gown over her and gave a low cry of alarm.

Then recovering, she said:

"Oh, it's you uncle?"

"Yes, my child, and I have accidently been a witness of your awful sin."

"Oh, uncle, I am very sorry!"

"Yes, I hope to make you!" he said. "Come here!"

"Oh, uncle, you won't hurt me, will you?"

"My child, I mean to whip the demon out of you!"

"Not whip me, uncle?"

"Yes, whip you, and I will have no more talking about it!"

He now takes the girl by the wrist and seats himself in the chair.

"Take off your dressing-gown!" he says, and helps her reluctance with a forcible pull that sends it on the ground.

"I must take off your drawers, dear!" he

goes on, as he lifts the chemise and fumbles round her waist and hips. Not finding the tie, he says:

"Come! Lie down over my legs!" He puts her over them and lifts the pendant chemise.

There over his thighs lies prone the form that he has so often wanted to see closely and examine.

Now, at last, his opportunity has come. He is not going to lose anything by being too hurried, so he smooths the drawers and strokes the dainty legs up and down slowly and deliberately. What whippings she shall have now that he has got her safe in his power, he thinks.

"Do you know," he says solemnly, "I might have you sent to prison for five years for what I saw you doing?"

She gives a sob in answer. "I must thoroughly frighten her," he thinks to himself, "if I am to do all I want to do without her saying a word to anybody."

"What is more," he says aloud, "if you do not submit without a murmur or a word to anybody to all the punishments I intend for you, I will inform the police!"

"Oh, I will tell nobody, I promise!" she

replies.

"Very well!" he says, all this while stroking her legs up and down and feeling the firm flesh with his fingers.

"Now stand up on that stool with your back to me." She obeys. "Lift up your chemise! Higher, up to your shoulders! That's it. Now bend over forward. More, more, I say! Open your knees wider! now bend further!"

She is now bent double with her drawers stretched tight over her bottom. He looks round for some weapon and takes a hairbrush. He lays it on the round left cheek of her bottom firmly, then raises it, waits a moment while she does not move and brings it down with a smart smack. He waits and repeats the smack on the same spot; then again harder, and once more still harder.

"Oh! oh! do the other side!" she cries.

"Not yet," he says, bringing another on the same place, then another. At this she lifts her body partly up; another smack and she is upright. "Bend down at once or I will send you to prison."

She bends down again, and he draws the covering smooth over the same place and goes on with some four or five more smacks.

Then he makes a pause and sitting down, pulls the girl over him and after several pulls and tugs gets her to his mind. He pulls up the drawers as high as they will go and feels the smooth white skin above the garters. He gets the drawers high enough to leave room for the back of the hairbrush on the skin and smacks first one thigh and then the other till the white turns pink. Then he tightens the drawers over the untouched cheek of her bottom and gives her some five minutes' whipping on it. Bidding her get up for a moment, he tells her to lie on the floor at his feet which she does on her face.

"Turn over!" he says.

She slowly turns half around; he seizes her and forcibly rolls her on to her back. The chemise covers her legs, but is loose in front and low cut. She pulls it up with her hands over her bosom which is delicately rounded with fast developing girlhood.

This immediately rouses his desire to see her breasts uncovered.

"Put your hands down at your sides! Obey me instantly or I will tie them together!"

She obeys. He takes the end of her chemise and gives it a pull downwards in front which pulls the top frill below her breasts, leaving them naked.

He rises and walks up and down behind her head where he can have a good view of her being half naked at his mercy. He keenly enjoys the prolonged sight of her nude little breasts. Presently he comes and sits over her. Gently he lifts the tails of her chemise and sees the front of her thighs encased in the white drawers. They fit almost tight. With the hairbrush he begins to smack them, just above the knee. In spite of herself, she cannot help twisting about. This gives him the excuse he wanted for placing his hand on her bare bosom to hold her. He however, determines to reserve the pleasure of taking off her drawers and baring her legs for another day's whipping. But he did everything short of that, that his fancy and passion suggested, and he ended by putting two chairs about two feet apart, making her straddle between them and hold up her chemise before and behind while he smacked the insides of her legs, pulling the drawers tight over the flesh.

He then told her to go to bed, but that he would give her more punishment another night.

Next day he satisfied himself on one of his pupils, making his wife strip her over a bed and cover her head with a blanket. In this attitude he whipped the girl for about half an hour while his wife went downstairs to finish teaching the others. He finds that when he is left alone with a pupil strapped down tight and practically blindfolded, he cannot resist being rather severe, particularly with girls that are too plucky to scream boldly, though when they do scream he always grasps the whip and gives four or five stripes with all his strength so as to raise marks on the instant right across the broadest surface. The girls knowing this (though they fancy it is his wife), soon learn to endure this whipping with only suppressed sobbings and imploring for mercy and much twisting, causing them always to be rewarded with strokes a little lighter. If they lie still, they find that the flicks are delivered smarter and smarter till they do wiggle about, so that the old pupils soon learn to begin twisting and writhing as soon as their feet and hands are fastened and before a stroke has been given. Sometimes they escape the whip for some minutes by sticking their bodies in and out and moving their muscles by arching their loins and then relaxing them, but all these tricks are unable to save them from ultimate chastisement which when once begun, has a way of steadily increasing in severity till the girl is nearly fainting.

In this way our curate found a week's satisfaction without again furbishing his niece. She was free from any marks of her former whipping when he stepped into her bedroom once more with a whip in his hand.

"Oh, uncle!" she murmured, "you are not going to punish me any more, are you? Indeed I am very sorry for what I did."

"My child," he replied, "the devil must be chastised out of you completely, and after the depth to which you have fallen, no punishments I can inflict are at all adequate, but my duty to do my best is clear. I only fear that I may err in being too lenient. My object to-night will be to humiliate you, and endeavour to awaken in you the shame that your immodesty has put to sleep. With this purpose I intend to strip your garments off one by one until you are completely naked and when quite nude, I shall make you stand before me in different attitudes for the space of half an hour. I hope this will rouse some shame in you. I shall whip you afterwards, and my severity will depend upon your obedience as to the attitudes I put you in. So first come here close to me and let me undress you."

With pouting lips, she sulkily goes to him, and he begins to undo her dress at the neck and down the front, slowly unfastening each button and at last pulling it off her white arms and drawing it down to her feet. He finds the next garment is a white calico body which he removes. Next come little stays and petticoats tied over them. Turning her round with her back to him, he unties the petticoats behind and draws them down. The tails of her chemise then appear. She is turned round again facing him and her stays are undone in front, her consent being given reluctantly.

This done, there only remain chemise, thin jersey drawers and stockings.

The chemise is short, reaching halfway to

the knee.

"Stand up on that stool!" he says. "Take off your shoes and stockings." He sits below while she bends and gracefully pulls off her stockings.

"Now come down here again."

She obeys. He quietly pulls up the chemise over her head, leaving only drawers and jersey. Her figure is beautiful in this scanty covering, and he cannot help showing eager haste as he tells her to pull off her jersey. She whimpers and does not move. He takes the whip.

"Off with it!" he cries, and delivers a stripe over the legs.

Up go her hands and off flies the jersey at once.

He now makes her stand on a low stool.

Her loins are on a level with his head. One button behind secures the drawers. He loosens it and they fall apart exposing the white posteriors and legs and the rounded thighs in front. Though her breasts are full and firm, she is almost without any hair on her body beyond her head.

Seating himself behind her, he orders her to turn very slowly round and round on the stool so that he can feast his eyes on her stark naked body. He makes her do the same on one leg with one foot in her hand. Next she had to twist about in the most lascivious contortions he could think of, and after varying them for half an hour, he, still making her present herself in these contortions, whipped her first gently here, there, and anywhere and at last with the utmost severity, making the whip lick round her shapely legs with quite a loud smacking sound. He at last takes her and lays her in the bed where he smacks her over the back and legs with his open hand for about ten minutes, after which he goes off to bed himself in a high pitch of excitement.

Finding his wife just preparing one of the girls for a whipping, he pretends to retire again while she blindfolds her; he then comes back with his shoes off and sits down to watch. His wife takes off the girl's clothes down to her chemise and drawers, and then fastens her hands to a hook in the ceiling. She then signs to her husband that he may hold the chemise up and pull the drawers tight over her loins while she whips her, this he does at once enjoying her twists and contortions as the whip descends with the steady precision of a woman who knows how to flog thoroughly. He soon finds that he longs to add his severity to hers. She notices his eager gesture to her to give him the whip, and does so. He gives a flick or two and then makes a pause. Taking the chemise, he pulls it over the girl's head; then he unties the drawers and pulls them off. He clearly likes whippings on the naked flesh best.

But the soft parts between the legs are what he wants to get at, so with strong twine, he fastens her strap garters to the ring on the opposite sides of the wall and with great force shortens the strings alternately until her knees are pulled apart farther and farther and her waist comes almost entirely on her hands. Then he takes up the whip again and aims stinging strokes between the straddled legs, attacking all the soft white places until his excitement is intense, voluptuously stirred with the victim's struggles and cries until at last he is satisfied and goes to bed and to sleep.

Not long after this, he was staying with a lady of about thirty who had married a widower. She had two stepdaughters. The eldest was nineteen and the youngest fourteen. The widower had recently died and the curate thought it a fine opportunity to teach the widow the pleasures of whipping.

The lady had never attempted such a thing, mainly from fear of her husband but that was now removed. Knowing the parson's wife whipped her pupils, she thought he would tell her how his wife managed matters. After luncheon, they walked out together and he began to talk.

"Those girls seem rather pert. Do you never punish them or take steps to make yourself properly feared and respected?"

"Well," she answered in a confidential tone, "I have often wished to make them treat me with more respect, but their late father would not allow me to punish them."

"How foolish! But it is not too late yet to bring them into subjection."

"Would you — whip them?" she suggested.

"Certainly!" said he, "in the most approved manner, — I would tie them up! And strip them properly and whip them thoroughly till they were completely docile and obedient to every word I said!"

"Will you assist me?"

"Indeed, I will with the utmost pleasure."

"When shall we do it? The servants would hear them cry out, I am afraid."

"To-morrow is Sunday," he said. "Do it when all the servants are at church. Order Mabel to stay behind in her room at the top of the house. Tie her hands and feet and blindfold her. Then I will come and help you."

So those two could hardly sleep for the anticipation of the next morning's amusement.

Mabel, delighted to escape the trip to church, went up to her room, presently followed by her stepmother armed with leather straps. The curate was to bring the whip.

"Mabel, dear," she said, getting behind her, "give me your hands. I want to try and experiment with these straps." The girl put her hands behind her in blissful ignorance of what was coming. She soon repented it.

The lady tied her wrists firmly together. Stooping down, she did the same with the ankles.

"Now, my dear," she went on, "I am going to punish you for all your rudeness and coolness to me!"

"What?" cried the girl. "How dare you!" She struggled to get free, but in vain. The straps held their victim tight. Taking an elastic cap she pushed it on over Mabel's eyes, completely blindfolding the girl.

She opened the door and the curate stepped in without his shoes, whip in hand.

"Undress her first," he whispered, putting down the whip and looking with cruel eyes at the delicate form of the girl.

"Shall I?" she said.

"Yes, of course!" he whispers and begins himself at the front of the dress over the bosom which he deliberately exposes to view as far as the close-fitting stays would permit.

The girl bent forward, hoping to shield herself from the exposure, but of course this gave a better view of her breasts, as her hands were secure behind.

The lady blushed scarlet, but feeling that she was committed now to the thing, whatever came of it, determined to enjoy it, and with trembling fingers drew the dress off the girl's white shoulders, bringing her laced chemise into view. But now a difficulty occurred as the hands were tied together. At a sign from the curate, one of the girl's hands was additionally secured to the bedpost. Then the other was undone and held tight by him while the sleeve was passed over it. Afterwards fastened with string at full stretch across the room to the window. The lass now stood in her stays and petticoats with arms outstretched. Her knickers were then unfastened, and let down to her feet till the calves of her legs appeared encased in silk and the frills of her drawers peeped from under the tails of the chemise. He now handed the lady the whip, and himself coming in front of the girl, pulled the chemise tight over her legs. The lady feels a mingled medley of pleasurable sensations as she brings the whip lightly over the tightened linen and observes the shrinking movements of the girl as she pokes herself out towards the curate who keeps the skirt tight all the time though not impeding her movements. After about five minutes, he signs to her to stop, but she adds a couple more smart strokes first; then he comes and lifts the pendant skirt and tucks it into the top of the stays behind; and while she again blushed scarlet, he lifts up the skirt in front and proceeds to push it down with his fingers, between the stays and the firm breasts. Coming behind her and leaning over her shoulder, he dives his hands down between and over her breasts with deliberation. The whipping recommences over the drawers, but after a while, he signs for a pause, feels for the tie and pulls them off to her feet leaving the white thighs naked. He now takes a paper knife from the table and stings the front of the legs while she continues her whipping over the posteriors. They strike alternately so as to make the girl dash her loins forward and back at each stroke. This gives her a most lascivious and abandoned appearance. Her twists presently loosen the chemise skirts, which fall down round her. A pause is made. At a sign from the curate, the lady unlaces and pulls off the stays. The chemise is cut very low and exposes the breasts and back as soon as the supporting stays are gone. The curate, taking some pins, rolls up the tails of the chemise behind and pins them to the low top, leaving only a roll round the small of the back. The whipping then begins again, each taking one thigh and leg to operate upon. Their excitement rises with the victim's cries and contortions. The lady at last seizes the front of the chemise and lifts it right up over the girl's head, leaving nothing on her from neck to knees. Then grasping the whip, she delivered about twenty strokes over the front of the thighs with all her strength.

The girl is now in a fainting condition, so the curate retires and the lady is left alone to unfasten her and remove the cap. The girl is ordered to dress herself and stay in her room till tea-time and left to herself.

The lady then joins the curate who is so excited by what has passed that he at once exclaims:

"Now for Rose!"

This is the other sister. The lady is also in no condition to be squeamish about it and they at once arrange to take her to a garret after tea and treat themselves to a thorough whipping of the child. The curate suggests that she is too young for it to matter about his being present and assisting without concealment.

The lady accordingly after tea tells the girl to follow her and ascends to the garret.

The curate follows, and entering, shuts the door and locks it.

"Now my dear," says the stepmother, "your conduct of late has been so insolent that I have determined to give you a whipping with the help of Mr. Cortes who has kindly offered to assist me in bringing you to a proper state of subjection."

The girl turns white, then very red as she perceives the curate approaching her. He takes her two hands firmly in his and going round a broad table draws her over it. The lady at once raises the skirts and petticoats on to Rose's back, exposing the posterior encased in thin, close-fitting drawers.

While she is doing this, the curate after placing one hand on the back of the girl's neck to hold her down, gets on to the table and kneels over her back with one knee close against each side of her little waist facing the lady. When the girl moves, he simply sits down heavily on her shoulders pinning her to the table like a vice. He tucks the skirts away under him, passes his hands over the

33

globes before him, and says to the lady softly:

"Let us take turns. Shall I have the first ten minutes or you?"

"Happy thought! Let us toss for it!"

So they toss and the curate wins.

The lady places the whip on the table beside him and goes out. Left alone with his victim, he feels and smooths the thin covering till the girl begins to see that her punishment is not undertaken to correct her fault but to afford pastime and to indulge these two in their sensuality. This thought rouses in her a strange pleasurable feeling and she says to the man whose hands she feels moulding her thighs:

"If you won't hurt me very much I will do anything you wish."

"Will you promise," says he, "if I let you get up to adopt any attitude I command?"

"Yes, I really will!" she says.

He however, gives her a few swinging spanks before he moves.

Though much hurt, she cannot but feel some kind of enjoyment as she knows she is rousing his lusts. Presently he gets off her and orders her kneel on the table. She instantly kneels as desired.

"Stick it out!" he says.

She thrusts her bottom out and the small of her back down in such a manner that he perceives that her own passions are up and that she wishes to excite him.

He takes the whip and begins to flog her lightly at first but gradually increasing the stripes. She bears it in silence. He next determined to see her legs naked and feels for the tie of her drawers.

She says: "Wait a moment!" and unties them herself.

He pulls them down and exposes the lovely heaps of flesh. He feels her all round while she never winces nor moves. Then the whipping begins again and is continued for five minutes until the girl sinks over in an agony of bliss and turning her over on her back he concludes with five or six strokes over her front with all his strength.

He then tells her to get up and put herself tidy, while he opens the door and calls softly for her stepmother who quickly appears.

The girl goes to him and says in a low voice:

"I would rather be whipped by you ever

so much than by her, the beast!"

But he feels bound to see the lady have her fair share, and also feels that it will be sport making the girl submit. So he replies that she must obey the stepmother. The latter lady is in no mood to forego delicious pleasures and requests the curate to take her over his lap. He therefore takes the girl firmly, and seating himself on a box, lays her over his knees. The lady lifts the skirts and he smooths the drawers for her. The whipping begins once more; gradually the shrinking and wriggling girl gets between his legs. He lowers his knees and leans back, holding her firmly to him. As the strokes fall on her bottom, she presses her front harder and harder against him while he meets each push of hers with an upward thrust of his thighs until all three actors in this strange lascivious scene are so carried away as to disregard all pretence of decency. The woman flogs, the girl wriggles and pushes and the man hugs and clasps the girl; each in the most abandoned manner until all three are at the climax of lust. At last, actuated by one instinct, the woman with trembling fingers pulls off the girl's drawers while the man undoes his clothes.

Clasping her close, he takes advantage of her warm contact in a manner that she cannot repel if she would. The cruel whipping begins again and the girl's loins press down with each stroke of the whip on to the man who receives the hot thrust with firm resistance until at last the two lie panting, one with pleasure and the other with pleasure and pain.

The ice was now fairly broken between the three and the curate knew that he was safe from any exposure, as the lady and her stepdaughter were too deeply compromised to have any further scruples. The curate, after this, used to go over regularly every Saturday and spend the afternoon in whipping the younger girl in every imaginable manner and with every possible concomitant of stripping and even nakedness combined with all varieties of attitude that could be suggested by this lust for his enjoyment. Meanwhile the poor girl began to find the excitement and pain and strange feelings rather exhausting and one day she begged that her sister might be served up for punishment in her stead. The change rather tickled the curate's fancy, so she was watched to her room and there visited by the three. She made a dart for the door, but her sister tripped her up and she fell on to a sofa. Instantly her sister jumped on her back and secured her hands behind her which the others strapped together. A handkerchief was stuffed into her mouth, and she was fastened tight over an ottoman. Her sister entreated to be allowed to give her a few stripes, which was granted. Her clothes were lifted and drawers lowered, and each took a turn of twelve strokes as a preliminary. Her frantic struggles amused her tormentors, and the curate suddenly felt that this girl pleased him better in having her own feelings of lasciviousness un-awakened by whipping, and with the whip in his hand and the writhing naked loins before him his pleasure in delivering the most cruel stripes seemed to exceed what he had experienced in whipping the other girl.

To test it, however, he presently made the younger girl stand over a chair, ordered her to lift her own petticoats over her shoulders and hold open her own drawers, all of which commands she instantly obeyed in a manner that showed how she revelled in the sensual pleasure of being subjected abjectly to the man's will.

He then whipped her till by her movements it was clear that she was in a paroxysm of excitement. He then returned to the elder girl and flogged her smartly while she struggled furiously and cried and exhibited no emotions but rage under the agony she suffered. His conclusion was that to whip one who angrily resented it, carrying with it, as it did, a greater sense of despotic power over the tightly-secured body of the girl, was on the whole the greater enjoyment of the two.

He therefore turned the others out of the room leaving him with the elder girl strapped down alone. When they were gone, he came and stood over the girl and said:

"Would you like to be whipped like this naked?"

But in a tone of intense fury she only muttered something about his being a brute.

Flick went the whip across her plump naked bottom with a sharp crack:

"Won't you answer civilly?" Another flick. "Do you like being stripped of your drawers by a man?" Flick! Flick! No answer, but the muscles contract fiercely where the whip strikes. "Would you like me to strip you altogether naked?" Crack! Smack! "Because I am going to undress you presently."

Swipe! A pause, then quickly and very severely: flick! flick! smack! swipe! "Obstinate girl, aren't you?" Swipe! swipe! over the tortured bottom.

"Ah! arr-he!" she yells at last. "You fiend! You monster! You devil incarnate!"

"Oh indeed!" he replied, laying the little whip carefully and firmly over both globes of her lovely behind and then with all his strength making the lash curl round them with an awful slash that made the blood at last appear.

The girl screams and writhes and drags at her bonds in her agony.

The curate now unfastens her so that she can get up with her hands still securely strapped together behind her back.

He unties her feet together so that she cannot kick or resist in any way, and then proceeds to undo her clothes with deliberation, and strip her, taking her things off one by one and undoing her hands when necessary, all with no hurry till she is stark naked. He then put a strap round her waist and strapped her wrists to it in the small of her back.

Finally he put a stick with rings at its ends between her feet and, with straps round her ankles, forced her feet a yard apart.

Her bottom was striped with weals and spotted with blood, but everywhere else she was a lovely cream colour. She showed no signs of voluptuousness. She continued furiously abusing the curate who, whip in hand, looked his victim over with gloating eyes.

"You are displaying a temper as naughty as your body is naked," said he, "and it is my duty as a clergyman to punish you till you are ready to be completely obedient, and the longer you resist the more humiliating will be the orders that I shall give you. My saintly office will nerve my hand to necessary severity."

And he suddenly swept the whip across the front of her large naked left thigh high up, making the tip of the whip lick round between her legs, and cut into the soft inside flesh. The poor girl howled and gasped from the fearful cut, which left a scarlet line on the white skin. With her legs held forcibly apart and her hands tied behind her, she could do nothing to defend herself, and the curate could aim cuts at every inch of her naked body and limbs without hindrance of any kind. Had there been any spectator, the completely-dressed parson whipping a stark naked girl would have presented a most startling and lust-provoking picture.

"The clergy so seldom do their duty like this," said he, cutting her again over her white thigh in front. "Girls would be much improved by an occasional whipping properly carried out like yours is now being performed." He flicked the lash well up into the gap between the girl's straddled legs.

At this the girl bent down as far as she could to try and protect herself from being struck up between her legs in front, but she forgot that this attitude would present her already well-flogged bottom tightly stretched. The curate seized the opportunity to slash the whip well across the already striped behind. This brought her smartly up again, while she struggled in vain to get her hands down to protect her posteriors.

Again he flicked the little whip between her naked thighs in front with a drawing cut that made her whole body jump. Then he waited, watching her twists and jerks and listening to her cries and sobs.

"I mean to whip you," he said, "until you are absolutely conquered, and are ready to submit without murmuring to any humiliation or degradation I may demand of you, but the longer you take to be brought to that state of abject subjection and humility the better I shall be pleased, for the longer I shall enjoy the pleasure of whipping you naked with ever-increasing severity."

With that he swiped the whip across her lovely white shoulders two or three times in quick succession, making her arch her back in and her large voluptuous breasts out in a very abandoned contortion. Then suddenly, without warning, he whisked the whip fiercely up across the lower curves of her firmly extended breasts.

An awful howl came from the victim when she felt this excruciating cut of the whip over the tender flesh of her bosom. The curate's lusts were becoming almost ungovernable from the excitement of this exquisite flogging of the helpless big girl.

His own loins moved to and fro in imitation of the girl's writhings.

"I shall master you yet, my girl!" he cried excitedly, "if I have to flay the skin off your pretty person!" and he cracked the whip downwards across the dancing breasts.

The girl once more bent forward, but as her hands were strapped tight in the small of her back, she could in no way protect her front. Her attitude presented her breasts downwards quite exposed to smart upward cuts of the whip which the curate proceeded to administer in the most cruel manner, striking the lovely globes fiercely over their centres with ever-increasing severity. At last, after a frightful cut that drew a spot of blood from the soft skin, the girl cried in a broken voice:

"Oh! Stop! Stop! Have mercy! I will obey you!"

"Are you quite sure you are conquered entirely?" he cried, with a frightful slash up between her thighs from behind, the tip of the lash licking round in front.

"Oh my God, yes! What do you want me to do?"

He put a pillow on the floor. "Kneel down on that!" he commanded.

The poor girl humbly knelt down sobbing, weeping; completely cowed and humbled.

The curate unfastened her hands and came and stood just in front of the naked victim. He leant back against the edge of the heavy table and told the girl to come close to him. He still held the terrible whip in his hand, touching her naked skin here and there with it lightly to accentuate his tyranny over her.

"Now you shall learn to serve me in every conceivable way I can invent for my own unbridled lusts and your utter humiliation. The more it horrifies you, the more delight I shall experience; you shall learn in the most intimate manner all the functions of the sexual organs of mankind, and you shall see the physical effects upon me that torturing you produces. Now uncover me, and from your own unblushing immodesty add to my sense of absolute domination over you."

The poor girl feels the whip laid down her

naked back ready for a smart cut, and she hesitates no more. With sudden, utter abandonment to her fate, she quickly unfastens the buttons just in front of her face, and draws apart his trousers. Without a pause, she puts her hands in and pulls the shirt away till everything is exposed, then she clasps his erect member with one soft hand; passing the other underneath and gently stroking and tickling him about. Keeping the whip against her white back, he watches her manipulations, sitting on the edge of the table and widening his thighs to grant her every facility.

Her soft hand strokes him slowly up and down giving him exquisite sensations.

"You must do still more for my pleasure," he says, pressing her pretty little head towards him with one hand and holding her down to open her mouth with the other.

At this the girl hesitated, pretending not to understand what was expected of her.

Up rose the whip and down it swept with a frightful slash all along her naked back, the knotted tip striking with a loud crack on the large bottom.

"Oh, my God!" groaned the agonised girl.

"Stop! Stop! I will do it!"

In an instant he felt his member clasped in her soft warm mouth; the knob gently sucked and pressed by her soft tongue.

The curate shut his eyes and turned his head up to the ceiling in the excess of his physical sensations.

He pushed her head firmly down and drove on right into her mouth, against the hot soft back of her throat, nearly choking her. Although her utter horror of what she was doing and being done to her was beyond all description, her terror of the whip in the man's strong hand pressed on her soft, naked flesh was greater.

"Work your head up and down steadily," he gasped. "Or I will flog the flesh off your back!"

And he gave her a playful flick to remind her of her risks. At this, the unhappy girl gave up all modesty and began sucking and exciting him with real desire to satisfy him and save her back.

Fingers, mouth and tongue were all at work, while he sat and absolutely groaned with pleasure with head thrown back and loins thrust out.

Nothing could exceed the strangeness of the scene: the curate, with trousers opened and his member deep in the mouth of the stark naked girl, who pressed up and down alternately exposing and then almost swallowing his enormous organ; the whip being held constantly against her soft flesh to enforce her abject service.

Then after a time, he called a pause, whipped her daintily and then ordered her to resume her provocations, till at last he began pushing fiercely into her himself and flogging her unmercifully at the same time, till with one last lunge, he consummated his lusts against the back of the throat, holding her head firmly to him with both hands.

(End of the Manuscript.)

CHAPTER II

CHAPTER II

After reading this most salacious description, Mr. Howard told Maud to fetch Miss Mary Hullah to the gymnasium. He was roused himself to a great pitch of lasciviousness by the perusal and awaited Miss Hullah's arrival with delightful anticipation. Presently she arrived with Maud. She was already half prepared by Maud who had dressed her only in a thin chemise and drawers under a loose silk dressing gown.

"I am glad to see," said he, "that Maud has prepared you for punishment, Miss Hullah. I have read the Ms. which was found secreted in your drawer, and the possession of such a piece of writing in your own handwriting is a fault of so unpardonable a kind that I feel it will be necessary to administer a chastisement to you that you will remember to your dying day. Moreover, the contents of the Ms. prove that no humiliations of a sexual nature I devise for you can possibly be unfamiliar to you. Now to begin with, I will give you your choice of being punished in Maud's presence and with her assistance to bind you and render you helpless, or of being left alone with me. If you choose the latter, you must promise absolute obedience to every order I give you, and the slightest rebellion will lead to your chastisement being repeated entirely to-morrow. Which shall it be?"

The picture of delicious maidenhood, Mary Hullah stood trembling before him. Without raising her eyes from the floor she said in a low voice:

"I will obey you, Sir."

"Absolutely?"

"Yes, absolutely!" she answered.

"Maud, leave us!" said he, and with a disappointed air, Maud slowly went out.

Mr. Howard lowered a trapeze to about a

foot above Mary Hullah's dainty little head. Then he placed her beneath it and said:

"Remove your dressing-gown!"

A very few buttons secured the loose garment and it fell around her to the ground.

The chemise had sleeves that buttoned on the top of each shoulder. It was very thin and scarcely concealed the lovely contours of the girl's pretty breasts.

"Take hold of the trapeze with both your hands!" said he. She obeyed at once.

"Now stand with your feet a yard apart."

Again she instantly obeyed, blushing scarlet.

Mr. Howard now drew the chemise this way and that tight over her body and legs, indecently shaping out her lovely form.

"Do you feel properly ashamed of yourself being inspected half naked by me?"

"Oh, Sir, I know I deserve it all, but I will try and please you if you will spare me the whip."

"You can't please me voluntarily in any way. I am not going to demand if I choose, and part of my pleasure is to whip you after I have stripped you slowly."

With that he quietly untied one of the

shoulder straps of the chemise and gradually laid bare one of her beautiful breasts. Then he daintily stroked it and moulded it in both his hands with slow deliberation while the poor girl panted with her agony of shame but said nothing.

Presently he untied the other shoulder strap of the chemise and gently stripped the trembling lovely girl stark naked down to the band of her drawers. The white dainty breasts were now laid bare under his wandering hands.

Nothing could exceed their loveliness; large and firm they rose and fell with the girl's excited breathing, rousing Mr. Howard's lascivious sensations to the highest pitch. Coming in front of her presently, he pressed her naked bust against him while he pushed one knee up between her separated thighs and felt her voluptuous bottom with one hand, squeezing and moulding its splendid contours through the tight silk drawers which were her only covering.

"Kiss me!" he commanded and Miss Hullah meekly pressed her soft mouth upon his.

"You are a sweet girl," he said, "and it is a pity that I must chastise you."

"Oh, don't whip me, dear Mr. Howard, please!" (She kissed him.) "Please don't. I will love you or do anything if you will let me off!"

And again she pouted her red lips into the softest, naughtiest kisses imaginable.

"I will love you a little first!" he said, letting her go on kissing him and pressing against him while he prepared the way and let her take his tool in her warm hand and direct it between her trembling thighs.

"As you have let go the trapeze without leave," he said, as he thrust firmly up into her, "I shall have to remember your disobedience by and by, but at present you are only postponing what is inevitable."

After remaining buried in her for some time, enjoying her sly efforts to excite him to a climax, he suddenly withdrew and took off his coat and waistcoat.

Approaching the girl once more, he untied the band of the drawers with careful deliberation, pushing them down off her glorious bottom and legs till they reached her ankles and lay across the intervening space on the floor.

After a long gaze at her exquisite body stripped naked to her garters, he rolled up the shirtsleeve of his right arm and took up a long, straight, narrow birch.

When she saw this, the girl began the wildest and most abject supplications for mercy. She promised to do or suffer anything if he would only let her off.

For all answer, he warned her that if she again removed either hand from the trapeze or brought her feet an inch nearer each other the entire punishment would be repeated from the beginning on the following week.

Coming straight behind his naked, trembling victim, he laid the birch across the right cheek of her snowy posteriors.

After one or two touches with it to perfect the aim, he let it slip and slashed the birch across the white flesh with a frightful cut.

The girl seemed almost choked with her agony; she threw up her head and screamed wildly.

Mr. Howard watched her and listened to her screams with a settled look of lust.

Changing hands, he presently smashed the flying twigs across the opposite cheek of her dancing bottom. Her cries were piercing, but she did not dare alter her strained position.

Again he paused and gloated over her trembling nakedness. Taking the birch again in his right hand, he measured the distance by putting the twigs up between her straddled thighs and with all his might slashed the birch up into the tender spot.

The whole body of the girl gave a frantic jerk accompanied by a shrill shriek of agony.

With set determination and sparkling eyes, and without saying a word to her, he followed these three cuts with three more similar ones: one right, one left and one up between. He seemed to be trying all he could to force her to be disobedient and alter her attitude. But in spite of her awful predicament, the girl remained with her hands above her head and her legs wide apart.

Six times he slowly and cruelly repeated the three frightful cuts; then, as her howls were turning to groans and sobs, he took up a fresh birch and came round in front of his wriggling, trembling, sobbing victim.

First across her right thigh and then

across her left, he swept the flying twigs, eliciting fresh screams; then, with the full strength of his arm, he whacked the birch right up between her lovely thighs.

With a writhing motion, the unhappy girl glued her legs together, unable any longer to obey the order not to move. This was really what Mr. Howard was trying to force her to do.

"How dare you disobey me?" he shouted in simulated rage. "Open your legs immediately!" But the poor girl still held them tightly crossed one over the other. "Very well," he cried. "You force me to severe measures. Until you obey me and put your feet a full yard apart, I must whip you on a more sensitive part of your naked body."

With a fierce flick, he whisked the flying twigs across the girl's left breast, striking the white surface with such force as to make the whole bosom jump with the impact.

All that had gone before seemed endurable to Miss Hullah compared with this fearful cut on her tender sensitive bosom. She felt as if a thousand scorpions and wasps were all stinging her there together. It was only by the utmost effort of will that she still held on to the trapeze at all. Mr. Howard placed the birch against her left breast preparing to strike a second time on the same spot. That so terrified the girl that she cried out:

"Oh, no! Not again for God's sake! I will open my legs! I will! Oh, stop!"

She separated her feet till they were straddled once more wide apart.

He obedience seemed to please her tormentor, for he placed the birch against the side of her loins and patted her as a coachman does a favourite horse.

He gloated over her naked body and legs stretched indecently apart. Miss Hullah was so frightened of the birch on her bare skin that she almost forgot the shame of standing naked before a man.

But Mr. Howard's lusts urged him on to continue the cruel whipping of the poor girl, and once more he slashed the birch across each of the girl's hips and then whisked it fiercely up between her legs. Her sobs and howls were heartrending and showed how terrible was the punishment. Little spots of blood were now appearing both on her hips and between her thighs.

Mr. Howard came and stood at her side and laid the long elastic instrument well across the whole of her large bottom which was still untouched and showed snowy white between the scarlet outsides of her hips, for the early cuts administered from behind had fallen over the outsides of the large cheeks of her bottom leaving all the middle of it unattacked.

He stood to her left with the birch in his right hand. Presently he struck with all his strength right across the firm white surface. The sound of the thump of the birch into the flesh was instantly followed by fresh screams and prayers for mercy from the writhing, wriggling victim. But Mr. Howard now was clearly past controlling his passions by any pity for the girl, and the birch fell again and again across her dancing, twisting posteriors with tremendous force, cutting through the tender skin and bringing beads of scarlet blood all about over the large, tortured surfaces.

Presently he took another birch and went round to the other side where, holding it in his left hand, he began again to slash across the already lacerated bottom from the other side.

He was now so excited that it was necessary to make a pause if a crisis was to be avoided, so temporarily putting aside the birch, he let down a rope from a beam in the roof of the gymnasium a little way from the trapeze and said:

"Now, Miss Hullah, you may let go the trapeze and I should like to see you swarm up that rope naked."

"Oh, Sir! I am only learning to swarm and have only once got halfway up to the roof."

"Capital!" he said. "We can combine instruction with chastisement. I will see whether I cannot induce you to swarm right up to the top which is about twenty-two feet from the ground. Come! Up you go!" And he flicked her naked legs smartly with the birch.

Miss Hullah ran to the rope, passed it round her naked right leg and began her ascent. Her twists and struggles made her look very tempting. Mr. Howard whisked the birch all about and over her struggling, naked thighs and body. Frantically the girl hauled herself a little higher and a little higher, till Mr. Howard could only reach her bottom by standing on a chair. With the awful birch flicking her naked legs, she exerted herself in the wildest manner and at last got out of his reach. She rested swinging slowly this way and that.

"Up you go!" said he presently, putting down the birch and taking up a carriage-whip: ten feet of handle and about twelve feet of lash.

When Miss Hullah saw what he held in his hand, she realised that he could reach her even if she got to the top and sat on the beam. Mr. Howard threw out the lash and, with an upward sweep, it struck the girl's plump bleeding bottom with the crack of a pistol. Long practice had made him an expert with a carriage-whip and he could hit a stamp on the wall with unerring precision if he chose.

The poor girl shrieked and almost let go in her agony. Then she made furious efforts to climb higher. Mr. Howard watched her struggles and waited till her bottom stuck out in her efforts to swarm up and then he slashed the lash right round the protruding flesh with a terrific cut.

The wildest cries and contortions were the result, but the poor victim's strength was failing at last and she could ascend no farther. She remained swaying about in her pain, crying for mercy, unable to go any higher and afraid of descending while Mr. Howard amused himself by aiming dexterous flicks at selected spots of her naked body and thighs. Her arms were of course stretched up above her head grasping the rope which came down between her lovely large breasts and passed through her thighs.

Mr. Howard threw out the lash and aimed a smart cut over the distended left breast. The corded lash struck the tender surface right across the pink little centre; the crack of the whip was followed by a howl of anguish, which would have moved Mr. Howard to desist if his lascivious sensations had not got complete mastery over him. The writhing, naked girl entirely at his mercy and the wicked carriage-whip in his hand precluded all emotions but his burning lust, and he followed up the last cut with one even more severe, aimed with perfect skill across the other lovely oscillating breast.

"You had better make an effort to get to the top!" he cried, slashing the whip with an awful swipe up against her lacerated behind, drawing the blood all across the large surface.

The girl once more began a wild struggle to ascend, but only succeeded in mounting about a foot.

"I can't go any higher, Mr. Howard, really! I am so exhausted I can hardly hold on at all!" the poor girl exclaimed between her gasps and sobs.

"Then come down and prepare for worse treatment!" he replied, slashing her over the front of her thighs with the long lash.

As the girl came down hand over hand, Mr. Howard cracked the whip round her wriggling body and limbs with fearful severity until she reached the ground and lay in a heap on the floor.

It was obvious that her limit of endurance was almost reached for the moment if the girl was not to faint.

Mr. Howard poured out some Champagne, put some brandy in it and made her take a good draught.

This seemed quickly to revive her.

"Put on tight silk drawers!" he said. "I do not like to see the marks all over your bottom and legs."

The girl rose up and obeyed him. As soon as the drawers were on, the white limbs looked spotless and tempting once more.

He now made her stand on a stool where she could just reach a trapeze hung from the top of the gymnasium, and ordered her to hold on to it firmly.

Then he took away the stool and left the girl hanging with her toes about a foot from the floor.

Coming behind her he gave her a steady push and started her swinging.

The trapeze being very long, she swung about twelve feet each way slowly and steadily. The stretch of her arms and body exposed every part of her tightly drawn frame. Once more he took up a long birch, and standing at the side of the swinging victim, began to strike her bottom and front alternately as she passed, keeping up her motion with the force of the blows. The poor girl shrieked at each cut of the flying birch, and her legs plunged and kicked in her agony, showing off their suppleness and lovely shape to perfection in the tight, white silk drawers.

With steady silence he kept the girl swinging for about five minutes.

At last he put down the birch.

"Now I shall reverse the operation," he said, "I shall swing you well up and then strike against the direction you are going till I bring you to perfect rest."

With that, he once more gave her body a big shove till she swung through quite a large area. Then taking up a lady's riding-whip, he whipped her bottom and front alternately as they came towards him, the motion of her body accentuating the impact of the whip. At the twelfth cut each way, he suddenly swept the instrument so fiercely over the silk drawers that they were cut through and blood appeared along the slit both in front and behind.

The sight of the girl's blood seemed to madden him, and regardless of all mercy, he slashed the whip across her shoulders and breasts, drawing blood once more.

The girl gave one long cry and letting go of the trapeze, fell to the floor in a swoon.

Fortunately the brandy she had taken

made her recover in a few moments, and Mr. Howard, lounging comfortably in a large arm-chair with the carriage-whip in one hand and lady's whip in the other, watched the helpless victim huddled in the middle of the gymnasium on the floor.

Giving her a little flick with the carriage-whip, he said:

"I have whipped you rather severely, Miss Hullah, but the result has been to rouse in me desires that I must now trouble you to gratify. Come here and kneel between my knees."

The girl, still sobbing, crawled humbly across to the spot indicated.

"Now as you have already so graphically described in your own handwriting what was done for the delectation of the curate, you must be good enough to execute the same arts and dexterities for my enjoyment, and if you really please me very much I will consider whether I will not let you off the renewal of your chastisement to-morrow."

"Oh! I should die if you flogged me again as you have to-day, I could not survive it twice!"

"Well then," Mr. Howard replied, "if you

want to live, you had better look sharp and I am sure I am more worth pleasure than any curate."

With that, he lay luxuriously back in the deep chair and presently felt himself being gently uncovered and most delicately manipulated by Miss Hullah's soft warm hands. She seemed to be perfectly skilled in the art of provocation of the passions. She drew the clothes away, lasciviously handling, grasping, tickling, and stroking him. Now and then she gently rolled his dart between her two soft palms, just touching the top of the nut with her pouting lips, producing the most insinuating sensations which made Mr. Howard fairly groan with intense delight.

"Stop a moment!" at last he murmured. "I wish to prolong my pleasure to the utmost."

At this, the girl opened her soft warm mouth and putting the whole of the shaft in till her lips closed round it, remained perfectly still against his body.

For full two minutes they remained thus motionless.

Mr. Howard's sensations were of the most exquisitely voluptuous nature. He could see both himself and the girl in a large mirror on his right, and they made a most erotic group with the naked girl humbly crouching between his widespread legs with her mouth glued to his body and his member completely engulphed in her mouth.

"Now go on again slowly!" said he.

The girl drew her lips up till they only remained the last inch of him, and her hands once more began to roll the shaft backwards and forwards between their soft palms. Several pauses and fresh provocations succeeded each other. At last Mr. Howard said:

"Now Miss Hullah, get up, sit astride of my thighs and take me into the right place."

Gracefully she rose and obeyed her master, first divesting herself of her drawers. He never moved and awaited her lascivious approach in a dream of lust.

Soon he felt her weight over his loins and delicious penetration into her delicious grove of love. He lay quite still leaving all motion to her. She was now sharing his sensations to the utmost and as she slowly rose and fell upon him, began to sigh with lovesick gasps. He told her to stoop enough to bring her lovely large breasts within comfortable handling distance, while he grasped them with both hands.

At last her movements began to accelerate and without further remonstrance from him, she began working up and down violently, her whole body joining in the voluptuous wriggling. Mr. Howard threw back his head and thrust out his loins, pinching her naked breasts at the same time in his nervous fingers, till at last the wildest paroxysm of lust overcame him and felt his very life pouring from him during a series of short lunges.

The girl now lay prone upon him and he allowed her to kiss his neck while she kept her lower parts tightly pressed down upon him.

They both lay throbbing with satiated passion.

"Why were you so cruel to me?" murmured the girl in his ear.

"You silly child!" he answered. "You would never have pleased me obediently or enjoyed yourself so perfectly if I have not first chastised you into abject obedience, besides the knowledge you must have possessed that it was lasciviousness and not cruelty that caused me to whip you, made it easier for you to bear, finally roused your own voluptuous feelings in an irresistible manner, and so rendering you most delectable as a little mistress. Of course, you were a naughty girl to write out all that most lewd story about the curate and therefore deserved your flogging. So now you may go off to bed and I will not whip again this term. But you must remember that I shall never enjoy you without a little preliminary chastisement which will have to be the price you pay for being permitted to revel in my embraces."

The girl now began to move gently up and down on him again, still panting with reviving lust, so vigorous in sweet eighteen. Mr. Howard's vigour was quite equal to a second flight with so lovely a girl tempting him in such an utterly abandoned manner. She hid her blushing face in his neck and sweetly moved her loins this way and that, giving him lovely sensations.

"Is this worth the whipping?" he said, giving a responsive heave that buried him in her vitals.

"Oh yes, yes, a thousand times yes!" she murmured in his ear. "I have forgotten all the agony I endured in the exquisite glory it is to lie in your strong arms, dear Lord and Master! You may whip me and torture me if only you will love me, too!"

This pretty speech pleased Mr. Howard so much that he clasped the soft girl's bosom to him and kissed her again and again till they were both throbbing and panting in a second satiation.

CHAPTER III

CHAPTER III

The subjection of Miss Hullah occurred towards the end of the summer term, and in a few days most of the girls departed for the holidays.

Miss Hullah being an orphan and taken in out of charity by Mr. Howard, was sent with one or two others in the care of an old servant of Mr. Howard to the seaside for six weeks.

Maud and Alice remained in charge of the empty school while Mr. Howard went for a few visits in Scotland. He returned however, a full fortnight before the reassembling of the pupils and finding only Maud and Alice at hand, made up his mind to treat them to a little of the old-fashioned chastisement which they had now for some time transferred from their own persons to that of their pupils.

Mr. Howard's early return rather disconcerted them as they knew his penchant for the whip and were rather afraid of what might happen in the interval before the return of the girls from their holidays. Although constantly assisting him at the chastisement of the bigger girls in the school, and also frequently whipping the smaller ones themselves, they had not been subjected to any punishment for quite six months. This fact, of course, added to Mr. Howard's pleasant anticipations, for he knew that the modesty of both the young ladies would have had ample time to become entirely re-established.

Both girls took good care to give him no excuse for finding the least fault with them and for a day or two they escaped by that means, but at last Mr. Howard made up his mind that he would just invent an excuse for punishing them.

He determined to begin with Alice and to administer just an old-fashioned straightforward whipping to the girl in the evening before she went to bed.

Suddenly ordering her to stand in front of him in the drawing-room after dinner, she came trembling from the piano in obedience to his orders.

"Lift up your skirts," he said. "Well above your knees, please."

Alice stooped down and obeyed him, lifting up all her skirts and laced underlinen exposing the frilled drawers.

"Ah!" he said, "I knew you would disobey me. I ordered you never again to wear those drawers."

"No indeed, you did not!" she whimpered.

"How dare you contradict me?" he replied. "I sentence you forthwith to fifty strokes with the riding-whip over those drawers, for your disobedience, and fifty more over your naked flesh for contradicting me. Go at once to the gymnasium. I will attend to you in five minutes."

With a half defiant toss of the head, Alice lets down her skirts, and walks gracefully out. The moment she was gone, Maud came over to her uncle and putting her hand on his leg, said:

"Did you see her toss her head? She deserves to be thoroughly whipped. Uncle, may I come to the gymnasium with you and help you to fasten her up? I may be of some use."

She said this coaxingly, well knowing that if not satisfied with Alice, she herself would have to suffer for his gratification and amusement.

"Very well," he said. "Go and take off everything but your chemise and drawers. Bring me the lightest of the ladies' riding-whips and come to the gymnasium. I give you three minutes. If you are late, look out!"

She fled in a terrible fright to her room, tore off her clothes and with sparkling eyes and heaving breasts, was in the gymnasium, whip in hand, almost before he reached it.

"I hope you did not crumple your dress in removing it, Maud?" he remarked icily. "I punish all untidiness severely, you know."

"Oh no!" she said. "I folded it carefully and put it away."

"Now then Alice," he went on, "stand there," indicating a spot where two rings were let into the floor fully a yard apart.

"Maud, strap her ankles to those rings."

Maud crouches down and fastens the feet wide apart.

The girl stood in this straddling attitude about a yard away from the wall in front of her.

Holding the whip delicately in his hand, Mr. Howard took his stand on one side of her and ordered her to take off her clothes.

Alice sees him flourish the little whip and feels a playful cut over her bare shoulders. Shrinking under it, she begins to undress with great haste.

"Not too fast!" he says, with another light flick this time over her bosom.

"Oh, how cruel you are!" Alice whimpers. "I cannot please you!"

"Oh yes, you do very much!" he said, swishing the whip about while she slowly removes first her dress, then her petticoats, and then her stays.

"At present," he continues, "you are stripped enough. Maud, hold up her chemise behind and please count in a clear voice the number of strokes."

Maud takes the chemise and lifts it up from over the lovely bosom and thighs, up to the band of the thin, close-fitting drawers. Alice awaits with straddled legs the beginning of her punishment. He handles the dainty whip a moment or two, feasting his eyes on the lovely, half naked lass trembling before him.

At last, he raises the whip and brings it smartly down over the garter. The girl gives a start and a scream and involuntarily struggles to free her feet. "One!" says Maud quietly, and holds the chemise a little higher. Up rises the whip and descends somewhat more severely about an inch higher up the leg. "Two!" says Maud.

Mr. Howard grasps the little whip tight and it fairly whistles through the air and makes an ominous crack over the plump surface of the leg about halfway up from the knee. "Three!" says Maud, while Alice's hands come convulsively to the whipped spot.

"Take away your hands!" says Mr. Howard calmly.

"Oh, uncle, have some mercy! Oh please let me off! You hurt so dreadfully!" cries the girl.

For all answer he flicks her naked arms to

make her take away her hands.

"Oh! Oh!" she screams. "Where may I put my hands?"

"Over the back of your neck and clasp them there!" he replies. "You had better be obedient, I warn you!"

She obeys and her hands are clasped behind her pretty little head.

Four, five, six, seven, eight, nine and ten, are then given with severity upon the same left leg. At the tenth cut, he pauses and tells Maud to furl up the chemise in front as far as her waist and to pin it there all round her body. This done, he signs to Maud to come and stand close by his side. She understands what is expected of her. As he delivers the first flick over the front of the left leg just above the garter, and as she says "Eleven!" she gently approaches him from behind and pressing against him, begins, with her arms clasping round him, to gently undo his clothes. As her warm hands mould and stroke the imprisoned member, he naturally grows more cruel, and with rapid crescendo the next ten stingers, all up the full plump thigh, are delivered and counted, Maud keeping time with her hands to the strokes.

At the twentieth, he crosses over to the other side of Miss Alice and the same cutting stripes are administered on the other leg, sometimes rapidly and sometimes slowly, as the soft up-and-down friction of Maud's hands bring him to the verge of a paroxysm. She counts in a clear voice up to the fortieth stroke.

"Now for her bottom, uncle!" whispers Maud in a sweet voice.

"Yes, yes!" he says. "Pin the drawers tight over the surface."

Maud leaves him and her dexterous fingers soon fix the thin cambric without a crease over the lovely swelling globes behind and on the dainty front. She comes back to her post. Alice's muscles jump and dimple in mortal fear as he lifts the little wicked whip. He pauses a moment watching her terror.

"Go on, uncle!" whispers Maud, her warm hands caressing him with the intention of bringing his cruelty to its utmost pitch.

"I will!" he says, and delivers a sweeping cut at right angles well across the centre of the two posteriors.

"41!" says Maud with a quick motion of her fingers.

Alice throws back her head and yells and struggles. Quick as thought follow 42, 43, 44 and 45. Maud counts in an excited voice while her hands fly softly to and fro losing all accuracy in their motions. Another short pause to cross over. Then disregarding screams and struggles and cries for mercy, 46, 47, and 48 given.

"Only two more!" says Maud, not stopping her strokings though he has paused. The baronet, beside himself, delivers 49 with all his might.

"49!" gasps Maud, her hands flying.

"Go on!" he says.

She obeys. He stands on tiptoe as the paroxysm approaches and delivers No. 50.

At a sign from him, Maud unfastens Alice's ankles and she is allowed to rest a few moments before the rest of the punishment is administered. Mr. Howard refreshes himself with a large glass of port, and allows Alice also a little fortification for what is soon to follow.

Presently he says quietly: "Take off your drawers, Alice!"

The girl obeys in silence, stripping off the last white covering and stepping daintily out of them. The chemise is still pinned up round her waist.

"Come and stand here," says he, indicating with the tip of his whip a spot in front of his chair.

"Sideways!" he says. "Now please stand still!" and he lays the whip to properly measure the distance over the two swelling globes of her now naked bottom.

Maud comes and crouches between his knees and gently uncovering and handling him, presses her soft moist, pouting lips warmly on the tip.

"Count only by fives now, Maud!" he remarks, still holding the whip against the trembling bottom. Suddenly the whip leaves the doomed surface; the girl sticks out her front in terror of the impending stroke which whistles through the air and fairly makes her jump from her position.

"How dare you move?" he cries, pointing to the original spot.

The girl silently gets again into position. Once more his aim is slowly taken and four sweeping cuts follow one another slowly and deliberately. Maud's lips are withdrawn a moment for her to say gently: "Five, uncle!"

Five more follow over the back of the legs, delivered very severely and without any haste.

"Ten!" says Maud, and returns to her task with mouth and fingers.

"Right about face, Alice!" says the baronet and poor Alice turns obediently round. He lays the little whip across her front, pressing the lash ominously in between the beautiful swelling white thighs that rise on either side of her *mons veneris* which has very little hair on it for a girl of seventeen.

"Oh, uncle, not there!" she cries, now sticking out her behind in mortal fear.

"If you don't stand upright immediately, I will strap you over the sofa on your back and double the number of your strokes," is all he replies.

And he gives her a swinging stripe.

"Now," he goes on, "if you want strokes no harder than that one, you must stick out your thighs in a forward manner each time to meet my strokes."

She actually meets the next flick with a

forward lunge of her hips. "That's right!" he says, enjoying her motions extremely. "Now again!"

She repeats it and he rewards her with a stroke almost playful compared to what has gone before.

At the fifth stroke Maud says: "Fifteen!" And soon "Twenty!" is reached.

He now gets up and orders Maud to fix Alice's feet once more to the rings in the floor a yard apart. Next, he orders the entire removal of the chemise, and lastly her hands are strapped together behind her back. He walks round her, feeling her here and there over her bosom and elsewhere; giving on every part of her little playful flicks that were not to count as proper strokes. Finally, Maud knelt before him and attended to him while the next 20 were delivered with the utmost severity over the front of the thighs. The last ten he aimed with all his force vertically between the wide-stretched legs.

After some more refreshment, Mr. Howard released Alice, but taking Maud by the ear he marched her off to her bed-room. There he found all her clothes, thrown off in her haste, lying in disorder about the room.

"Ah!" said he. "Untidy as usual, and a liar as well!"

"Oh, Sir, you told me to be done in three minutes! How could I fold up the things?" said the girl turning pink with fear.

"But you lied!" said Mr. Howard, locking the door. He still carried the riding-whip in his hand. "Undress! I think I will whip you in your nightgown. It will be a new costume for a flogging and can be easily removed if it does not please me."

Reclining on a sofa, he ordered the young girl to bring her nightgowns for him to choose from. She brought three or four.

"Kneel here!" said he. Kneeling humbly before him, she held out one nightgown after another for him to look at. He chose one made of transparent cambric, and ordered her to begin undressing on her knees by his side. As she obeys and begins to uncover her white shoulders, arms and bust, the baronet, with the flat of his hand, gives her a smack here and there making her hold herself appropriately to receive the spanks. When stripped naked to the waist, he made her bend backwards over his lap, and holding her back with one arm under her chin, he pinched the little pink nipples of her up-stretched breasts and spanked her shoulders and sides. Maud wriggled and cried out, but dared not really struggle.

Mr. Howard, having rendered himself sufficiently lascivious by these preliminaries, at last told her to put on the nightgown, and lay herself over his lap.

"Quick!" he said.

Maud, knowing how delay incensed him, was in the nightgown with everything else off and was over his legs in a trice. Her elbows were on the floor on one side and knees just off the ground on the other. Mr. Howard took the whip and proceeded to arrange the transparent covering tight over her legs, thighs and back without a crease. This he did with much deliberation.

"Fifty for the untidiness!" he remarked. "We will assess the punishment for the lies afterwards."

Her warm body pressed suddenly down upon his now stiffening yard as he brought the whip smartly over the doomed posteriors. Wriggle, wriggle, follows upon stripe, stripe. The tenth stroke he delivers with such force that the girl rolls off his knees on the floor in agony.

"I was foolish to suppose you would lie still without straps," said he, slowly rising and fetching a bundle of cords and straps.

"Oh! don't strap me, please! Don't strap me!" she cried, kneeling at his feet and clasping him round the knees in her fright.

"Eleven!" says he, bringing a stripe vertically down over her bottom.

"Let go of my legs! Twelve!" he continues, with another in the same place. She lets go of his knees.

13, 14, 15 follow, and while she remains kneeling, and writhing. 16.

"Stand up!" She stands. 17. "Hold your nightgown tight over your bottom and legs." 18. "Do it at once!" 19. "Do you hear?" 20. "That's right." 21. "Now let me see you work the muscles of your bottom well." 22. "I can see it beautifully through the thin covering." 23. "That's it!" 24. "Go on!" 25, 26, 27. "Now for a few real strokes!" 28, 29, 30. "Ah! Oh! Oh!"

"Hold your nightgown tight over your front now." 31. "Quick!" 32. "Better than that. No creases, please." 33. "That's better." 34, 35, 36. "Now pull it though between your legs, tight from behind." 37. Don't be so clumsy! Arrange it with no thickness or creases anywhere." 38. "That's more like what I want." 39, 40. "Now straddle your legs apart." 41. "Wider!" 42. "Wider still, please!" 43, 44. "Don't shrink away like that!" 45. "Here! Put your bottom against the side of the bed. Now lean back!" 46. "Farther back, please." 47. "You are very disobedient? Lean back at once." 48. "That's right!" 49, 50!

"Now you have had your punishment for untidiness, but lying is of course, a much worse fault and requires worse chastisement if I can devise it."

"Oh, dear uncle, don't whip me any more! I'll never lie again."

"No," he said, "lying is a serious matter. Go to the gymnasium and make Alice hang you up with the broad strap round your shoulder till your feet are a foot from the ground. Quick!" The girl tremblingly obeyed, while Mr. Howard, choosing a lady's whip and a coachman's whip with a long lash, followed at his leisure.

He found the girl suspended as directed, and he ordered Alice to furl the nightgown round the strap from above and below, leaving the girl entirely naked. Her arms and legs were now free to kick and writhe, and he looked the lovely body and limbs over with sparkling eyes. Presently he threw out the lash of the carriage-whip and swept it round the soft, white, plump legs.

The lash made a wicked crack over the naked skin, and immediately her legs launched out into every imaginable lascivious contortion while her screams filled the apartment.

Alice still stood meekly with no drawers on and her chemise pinned up round her waist, as she had been left by Mr. Howard.

"Come here, Alice," said he, "and sit astride my lap."

Sitting down where he could comfortably reach suspended naked Maud with his carriage-whip, he arranged Alice over his legs so that she could give him perfect sexual congress.

When the girl had got him buried to the hilt in her delicious warm body, she began undulating slowly and firmly in time with the sweeps of the whip as the thong licked round Maud's dancing limbs. Mr. Howard's dexterity was extraordinary with the lash and he slowly ascended the leaping, writhing thighs, slashing them with unerring precision higher and higher.

With each slash of the whip, Alice pressed down upon him, making him penetrate to her very vitals. She was now wildly lascivious herself and had lost all sense of shame or modesty. She looked over her own bare plump shoulder at the kicking legs of the suspended victim and watched the fearful whipping with rising lust.

At last the girl's legs are all striped with weals and the lash sweeps right across the lovely plump bottom with the crack of a pistol. As the victim shrieks and jumps, Alice feels Mr. Howard's manly member throb and stiffen within her in the extremity of his sensuality, and drinking in with delight the yells of the unhappy tortured girl, she glues her body with a fierce lunge against her master.

With rising and ungovernable lust, he grasps the whip and smashes a frightful cut right between the girl's naked legs in front.

This was followed by a choking howl of anguish and by vigorous oscillations of Alice's body upon her master's lap.

Maud frantically tries to protect herself by putting one hand between her legs in front and one over her tortured bottom behind.

Mr. Howard throws out the lash and delivers a frightful crack across her naked right breast, followed by a return cut up between her thighs behind.

But these excruciating lashes carry his lasciviousness beyond his control and with pants of excitement, he abandons all restraint and thrusting into Alice with might and main drops the whip with a last groan of repletion.

By and by he told Alice to get off him and let Maud down. Both girls were allowed to put on beautifully embroidered silk nightgowns and to cover themselves with lovely quilted dressing-gowns.

In that pretty garb the girls prepared a dainty supper for themselves and Mr. Howard.

Both lassies evinced the most abject desire to please their inexorable master, and no Sultan ever had more humble slaves to wait upon him.

They had both long ago learnt that the more they accentuated his unlimited power over them and the more they showed that they willingly concealed it, the more sensual pleasure he derived from their daily intercourse. Without being told, they served him with everything, kneeling on the floor beside him with each dish.

They both knew perfectly well that he would indulge himself in some more chastisements after supper, and each hoping to induce him to choose the other for the whip and herself for dalliance, used every art to tempt him to select her for the latter. Maud, as she served him, accidently allowed her dressing-gown to fall apart and show him her sweet rounded bosom under the smooth silk, not altogether uncovering it naked because of the marks of the whip which it bore.

But these artifices, though gradually rousing Mr. Howard's somewhat jaded passions, did not make him feel at all inclined to spare either of his captives.

When the meal was over, he proceeded languidly to give his orders. He directed Maud to lie down in the middle of the gymnasium and ordered Alice to fix the victim's wrists a yard apart above her head to rings in the floor. Her feet were then stretched very wide apart and strapped by the ankles to the ends of a bamboo stick which itself was furnished with rings at each end.

The rings were then attached to a pulley directly in the ceiling over the girl's hands.

The girl now lay on her back distended like a star fish. Mr. Howard approached her and opened the dressing-gown revealing her beautiful body, breasts, and thighs with only the thin silk to conceal them.

"Now, Alice," he said "elevate Maud's feet till she is inverted at full stretch."

The pulley was a double one which made it quite easy to raise the girl slowly and steadily into the required position. As her feet began to ascend, the night-gown gradually slipped up the black stockings till the garters came into view; then the plump naked legs; and at last, as the girl's body was lifted up and up, the silk fell away revealing everything to the chin.

"Pull her quite tight!" said Mr. Howard, and Alice, hauling at the double pulley, drew Maud's distended ankles tight till she was stretched quite immovable upside down with arms and legs pulled wide apart like a St. Andrew's cross.

The night-gown fell down and lay on the floor between her wrists.

Mr. Howard brought a chair close to the helpless girl and sat down, while Alice fastened the rope securely to hooks in the wall.

Putting one hand upon her inverted breast and the other between her thighs, he said:

"The knowledge of your complete helplessness under my hands is one of the chief sources of my sensual pleasure, Maud. The sense of your indecent subjection to my slightest whim gives me subtle physical pleasure, and that delight becomes exquisitely acute when I add the infliction of pain to your exposed tender flesh."

Here he began steadily pinching the soft skin of her bosom in his nervous fingers with one hand and presently thrust two fingers of his other hand into her tender gap. The unhappy girl could do nothing to protect herself, and though her body swayed a little as she tried to struggle, her cries for help were all that she could do to relieve herself under the cruel attack. Her cries excited him sufficiently to make him tell Alice to give him the riding-whip. As soon as she had handed it to him, he said to her:

"I cannot have you get in my way, but I intend to use you for my purposes, so put the arm-chair in front of me, and come and place yourself across my legs with your back to me and put your head into the chair."

Alice came and gracefully got astride of his thighs and while she began to lean forward, dexterously received him deeply into her and then lay forward till her head and shoulders were down on the seat of the chair, while her bottom and divided thighs were across his lap.

He lifted everything off the girl's naked bottom and back, and gave the big posteriors a smart cut with the whip which made her glue herself down to him with a fierce jerk which buried him deliciously in her warm vitals.

Turning his attention to his extended victim, he slashed the whip across her inverted behind. When Alice heard the crack of the whip she pushed her loins down upon Mr. Howard while Maud screamed with pain.

"Oh, why should I have to bear it all? Have mercy on me!" cried poor Maud, trying to writhe about.

"You are not bearing it all!" said he. "I am now going to make Alice join her shrieks to yours." He took up a bunch of gorse and holly leaves and place it against the naked bottom across his lap.

Alice, when she felt the first touch of this fearful instrument, gave a startled cry and pressed her bottom down upon him. He leant back a little in his chair, pushing his own loins up to meet her downward pressure, and then he began tapping her naked behind with the prickles; each tap producing wild and fierce downward lunges of her loins and louder screams.

Presently he returned to Maud and struck the whip smartly across her naked breasts and while she swayed and screamed, he allowed Alice to lie still upon him so as not to hurry matters too much.

Finding it difficult to do justice to the opportunities afforded by the inverted naked girl while he sat down in the chair, he once more turned his attention to Alice, who was lying quite still with his tool buried deliciously in her.

Raising the bunch of holly and gorse, he dashed it down across the girl's naked loins, producing a wild shriek and a fierce plunge of her thighs which she opened as wide as she could, forcing herself tightly against him. He met the plunge with a firm upward push of his own body which gave him the utmost physical delight. The girl, too, in spite of the dreadful pain of the bunch of holly crushing into her naked behind, felt the rapture of the fierce penetration in front. With cries and screams, beside herself with the extreme acuity of her confused and diverse sensations, she oscillated her loins up and down, opening her thighs to the utmost, in an utterly abandoned manner which so intoxicated Mr. Howard, that at last, with a groan of repletion, he dropped the instruments of torture and with a final upward lunge experienced the ultimate throb of exquisite bliss.

As soon as Mr. Howard had recovered from his delicious enjoyment of Alice, he seized a riding-whip in one hand and a long thin birch in the other. He was thus prepared to give Maud a unique thrashing.

He knew that after his dalliance with Alice, nothing short of prolonged severity would excite him afresh.

He bared his strong arm for the encounter and took up his position in front of the naked, suspended girl.

"Alice," he said, looking Maud's lovely body and limbs over with steady scrutiny, "go behind Maud and push her body towards me."

Alice immediately obeyed and thrust poor Maud's body into a curve which stretched her breasts quite tight in an abandoned forward contortion. She put her knee against the girl's shoulder blades and her hands against her bottom. She could watch Mr. Howard between the widely-straddled thighs. Seeing that he was measuring the distance to cut across the breasts with the birch, she pushed with her knee, protruding Maud's large globes to meet the attack.

Mr. Howard took careful aim and slashed the twigs across the firm surface. The thud of the birch was followed by frantic cries and prayers from the inverted girl. He took no notice and laid the whip into the crack between her legs. Alice withdrew her knee from Maud's shoulders and pushed her bottom with both hands till she had protruded the girl's loins in a tight immovable contortion, presenting the soft and sensitive region between her legs most temptingly. Mr. Howard tapped the spot several times with the tip of the whip, enjoying the spectacle of the exposed gap waiting for the stroke. He measured the distance exactly so as to secure that the knotted tip of the whip should penetrate well into the divided lips of the young girl's private organ. At last he raised the whip over his head and struck down with a fearful drawing slash making the knotted end hit with exquisite accuracy.

The blood spurted from the tender orifice; a shriek filled the apartment. He slashed the whip with all his might across the naked breasts and as the paroxysm of lust overcame him, he dashed the whip for the last time again between her thighs. Exhausted by his sensual exertions, Mr. Howard sank into a chair, and told Alice to let Maud down. They were then both ordered to go to bed where he would join them later on if he felt inclined.

With his satiety, he felt some regret for having so cruelly flogged Maud, but he remembered that she would probably revenge herself on some of the girls in the school later on, and that therefore she deserved to pay for own indulgences.

How Mr. Howard found the means to explore some even higher flights of sensuality will be recorded in another volume now in preparation.

THE END

NOW ON SALE :

WORKS BY THE SAME AUTHOR

Two Lascivious Adventures of Mr. Howard.
Price : £ 1.10.0.

Mr. Howard Goes Yachting (six illustrations).
Price : £ 2.2.0.

Fantastic Chastisements. . . Price : £1.1.0.

SHORTLY :

Exquisite Castigation. . . . Price : £1.1.0.

JUST OUT BY A NEW WRITER

Our Fair Flagellants, two stout volumes,
beautifully printed, with twelve illustrations,
limited issue.
Price : £ 4.4.0.

IN THE PRESS :

Rachel Rodskiss, by Barbary Birchenough.
Price : £ 1.10.0.

BIRCHGROVE PRESS
Flagellant & Libertine Erotica

More books and e-books from Birchgrove Press:

Charles Sackville:

Mr. Howard Goes Yachting
Two Lascivious Adventures of Mr. Howard
Three Chapters in the Life of Mr. Howard
The Amazing Chastisements of Miss Bostock
Fantastic Chastisements

Edwardian Erotica:

Miss Mary
Miss Grégor
Rachel Rodskiss
Our Fair Flagellants
Sadopaideia
Lashed into Lust
The Cruise of the "Water-Lily"

Victorian Erotica:

The Mysteries of Verbena House
Experimental Lecture by Colonel Spanker
Raped on the Railway
The Pleasures of Cruelty
The Haunted House or The Revelations of
    Theresa Terrence (1880 Christmas edition of
    The Pearl: A Journal of Facetiæ and
    Voluptuous Reading)

Pre-Victorian, Victorian, and later erotica:

Manon la Fouetteuse
Venus School-Mistress
The Birchen Bouquet
Flagellation and the Flagellants:
    A History of the Rod in all Countries...

The New Ladies Tickler
Miss Coote's Confessions
Lady Pokingham; or They All Do It
Flunkeyania; or Belgravian Morals
The Merry Order of St. Bridget
Rosy Tales!
The Romance of Chastisement

Memoirs of a Russian Ballet Girl
The Callipyges: The Whole Philosophy and
    Secret Mystery of Female Flagellation
Lady Gay Spanker's Tales of Fun and
    Flagellation
Woman and her Master
"Frank" and I

The Beautiful Flagellants of New York
    (three volumes in one)
Realistic Pleasures Gathered from the Diary
    of a Sybarite
The Revelations of Shrewsbury House
The Whippingham Papers

De Rhodès and Petticoat Discipline:

Gynecocracy
The Petticoat Dominant
The Yellow Room
Stays and Gloves
Miss High Heels

Library Illustrative of Social Progress:

*The Exhibition of Female Flagellants Parts
    One and Two*
Lady Bumtickler's Revels
*A Treatise of the Use of Flogging in Venereal
    Affairs*
Madame Birchini's Dance
Sublime of Flagellation
Fashionable Lectures
The Rodiad

American Twentieth-Century Classics:

Modern Slaves
Presented in Leather
Painful Pleasures
The Song of the Whip
The Unique Experiences of Flossa
The Strap Returns

Libertine Fiction:

Venus in the Cloister
The Dialogues of Luisa Sigea
The School of Venus
A Treatise of Hermaphrodites
Opus Sadicum

French Flagellant Fiction:

*Conférence Expérimentale par le Colonel
   Cinglant
Les Mystères de la Maison de la Verveine*

Aleister Crowley:

Snowdrops from a Curate's Garden
White Stains

Algernon Charles Swinburne:

The Flogging Block An Heroic Poem
(landmark first publication of the entire
cycle of poems from *The Flogging Block*
manuscript)

Non-Flagellant French Fiction in translation:

Pierre Louÿs:

The Songs of Bilitis
Woman and Puppet
The Twilight of the Nymphs

Gérard de Nerval:

Aurelia
Sylvie

Octave Mirbeau:

Torture Garden
The Diary of a Chambermaid

For a complete list of titles and formats, please visit our website:

www.birchgrovepress.com

www.ingramcontent.com/pod-product-compliance
Lightning Source LLC
Chambersburg PA
CBHW072003170626
46813CB00005B/1987